SPOT the Differences Christmas
Search & Find Fun

Illustrated by Genie Espinosa

Dover Publications, Inc.
Mineola, New York

Bibliographical Note

This Dover edition, first published in 2019, is a slightly altered
republication of the work illustrated by Genie Espinosa and
written by Lisa Regan, which was originally published by
Arcturus Publishing Limited, London, in 2019.

International Standard Book Number

ISBN-13: 978-0-486-83798-7
ISBN-10: 0-486-83798-X

Manufactured in the United States by LSC Communications
83798X01
www.doverpublications.com

2 4 6 8 10 9 7 5 3 1
2019

JINGLE BELLS

Jingle all the way to Christmas by spotting 10 differences between these two pictures. Circle the changes in the scene on the right.

HE'S MAKING HIS LIST

You better not be on the naughty list!

Spot 10 differences in the scene below and circle them.

TIME TO BE FESTIVE

Do you think there are enough decorations outside this house?

Find and circle 10 differences in the picture below.

DEAR SANTA

Writing letters and making cards at Christmastime is fun!

Can you find and circle 10 changes in the cute scene below?

BUSY, BUSY

Not long until Christmas, and still plenty of work to be done!

Find and circle 10 differences in the busy workshop scene below.

SWEET DREAMS

These two festive fairies are sprinkling Christmas cheer.

Find the 10 differences in the scene below and circle them.

A HELPING HAND

Kitty loves decorating the tree!
Circle 10 differences in the picture on the right.

ALL ABOARD

The Christmas Express is about to leave the station.
Spot and circle 10 changes in the picture on the bottom.

HAPPY HELPERS

Santa Claus is taking care of his animal friends.

Try to spot and circle 10 differences in the scene below.

SPECIAL DELIVERY

Christmas is a time for visiting friends.

Circle 10 differences in the happy scene pictured below.

SILENT NIGHT

Shh! Enjoy the peace.

How quietly can you find and circle the
10 changes in the scene below?

CUTE CAROLERS

Everyone loves to go caroling—even the pets!

Find and circle 10 changes in the picture below.

A CHRISTMAS CANDY COTTAGE

Yummy! This gingerbread house looks good enough to eat.

Can you spot and circle 10 tasty differences?

TASTY TREATS

Christmas baking is the best!
Circle 10 things that are different in the scene on the right.

A SNOWY SCENE

Santa Claus is all shook up!
Find 10 changes in the picture of the snow globe on the right.

ALL TOGETHER

Some jobs are easier when you have lots of help!

Find and circle 10 differences in the outdoor scene below.

DECK THE HALLS

This Teddy Bear family loves Christmas!

Find and circle 10 differences in the picture below.

WINTER WONDERLAND

All the animals are helping to pack up Santa's Christmas sack.

Look for 10 changes in the cute scene below and circle them.

WAITING FOR SANTA

All the animals are *trying* to sleep but they're excited for Christmas morning!

Find and circle 10 changes in the sleepy scene below.

LIGHT UP THE NIGHT

Ready . . . steady . . . lights!

Find and circle 10 changes below that will brighten your day.

WHITE CHRISTMAS

It's hard to spot the sheep in the snow!

Do your best to find and circle 10 differences in the scene below.

IT'S A WRAP

Wrapping presents is so much fun!

Find and circle 10 changes in the picture below.

PILE THEM HIGH

There are lots of colorful presents!
Find and circle 10 changes in the bottom picture.

IT'S SNOW TIME!

Let's head outdoors to make a snowman . . . or a snow animal!
Find and circle 10 changes in the fun scene on the right.

CHRISTMAS CROWDS

Everyone is out shopping and enjoying the sights of the season!

Spot and circle 10 differences in the busy scene below.

45

FUN AT THE HOLIDAY FAIR

There's so much to do at this Christmas carnival!

Find and circle 10 differences in the picture below.

IN A SPIN

Join everyone on the ice for a fun day of skating!

Spot and circle 10 differences in the scene below.

TWELVE DAYS OF CHRISTMAS

Surprise! In this puzzle, there are 12 differences to find.

Spot and circle 12 changes in the scene below.

ON THE SLOPES

Whee! Slip and slide before the snow melts!

Spot and circle 10 differences in the scene below.

ELVES ON SHELVES

The elves are decorating the house. Have you spotted all 10 differences?
Circle them in the scene on the right.

CHRISTMAS KISSES

Love is in the air at this special time!
Look for 10 differences and circle them in the picture on the right.

A STAR IS BORN

These little performers are putting on a Christmas show!

Find and circle 10 differences in the scene below.

FIRST WINTER SNOW

The snowy scene outside looks beautiful, especially at Christmastime.
Find and circle 10 changes in the scene on the right.

HOLIDAY PICTURE PUZZLER

These 2 pictures look alike, but they're not.
Spot and circle 10 changes in the image on the right.

THE NUTCRACKER

Pretend you're a part of this famous Christmas story.

See if you can find and circle 10 differences in the scene below.

TIME FOR BED

It's Christmas Eve—but who can sleep?

Find and circle 10 changes below before you close your eyes.

READY FOR TAKEOFF

Santa Claus is checking his list so he's ready for his deliveries.

Find and circle 10 differences in the picture below.

'TWAS THE NIGHT BEFORE CHRISTMAS

Some creatures are stirring on this Christmas Eve!

Spot and circle 10 differences in the picture below.

LOOK UP!

Get set, Santa . . . go! Can you see him in the sky?
Spot and circle 10 changes in the bottom scene.

A NORDIC NOËL

Here's a super-cool design you could find on a Christmas sweater.
Find and circle 10 changes in the design on the right.

FESTIVE FIREWORKS

Celebrate the holiday in Moscow's Red Square.

Find and circle 10 differences in the Russian capital below.

"GOD JUL"*

Swedish celebrations for Christmas start on St. Lucia's Day.

*"Merry Christmas" in Swedish

Can you spot and circle 10 differences below?

"FRÖHLICHE WEIHNACHTEN"*

Some German legends say St. Nicholas leaves good children presents in their shoes, but Ruprecht leaves a lump of coal for naughty children.

*"Merry Christmas" in German

Find and circle 10 differences in the scene below.

"FELIZ NAVIDAD"*

Spanish celebrations for Christmas continue until Three Kings Day.

*"Merry Christmas" in Spanish

Find and circle 10 changes in the scene below.

CHRISTMAS DOWN UNDER

In Australia, you might spot Santa and his sleigh being pulled by kangaroos!

Spot and circle 10 changes in the scene below.

"GLEÐILEG JÓL"*

Icelandic children receive presents from 13 Yule Lads,
who might play tricks!

*"Merry Christmas" in Icelandic

Find and circle 10 changes in the picture below.

PIÑATA PARTY

In Mexico, children celebrate Christmas by breaking open a piñata during nine days of celebrations called "Posadas." Find and circle 10 differences in the bottom picture.

GRANDPA FROST

Russian presents are delivered by Ded Moroz and his granddaughter, the Snow Maiden. Find and circle 10 changes in the scene on the right.

A FESTIVE FEAST

The big day has arrived and it's time for a special meal!

Feast your eyes on the scene below and circle 10 differences.

LET'S PLAY

After dinner, it's time for a game.

Spot and circle 10 differences in the family scene below.

PARTY TIME

Enjoy all the celebrations before the holiday season ends!

Find and circle 10 differences in the scene below.

MERRY CHRISTMAS!

And finally . . . wishing you a Merry Christmas from everyone!
(Don't forget to find and circle the 10 differences in the scene on the right!)

ANSWERS

3 JINGLE BELLS

4-5 HE'S MAKING HIS LIST

6-7 TIME TO BE FESTIVE

8-9 DEAR SANTA

10-11 BUSY, BUSY

12-13 SWEET DREAMS

14 A HELPING HAND

15 ALL ABOARD

16-17 HAPPY HELPERS

18-19 SPECIAL DELIVERY

20-21 SILENT NIGHT

22-23 CUTE CAROLERS

24-25 A CHRISTMAS CANDY COTTAGE

26 TASTY TREATS

27 A SNOWY SCENE

28-29 ALL TOGETHER

30-31 DECK THE HALLS

32-33 WINTER WONDERLAND

34-35 WAITING FOR SANTA

36-37 LIGHT UP THE NIGHT

38-39 WHITE CHRISTMAS

40-41 IT'S A WRAP

42 PILE THEM HIGH

43 IT'S SNOW TIME!

44-45 CHRISTMAS CROWDS

46-47 FUN AT THE HOLIDAY FAIR

48-49 IN A SPIN

50-51 TWELVE DAYS OF CHRISTMAS

52-53 ON THE SLOPES

54 ELVES ON SHELVES

55 CHRISTMAS KISSES

56-57 A STAR IS BORN

58 FIRST WINTER SNOW

59 HOLIDAY PICTURE PUZZLER

60-61 THE NUTCRACKER

62-63 TIME FOR BED

64-65 READY FOR TAKEOFF

66-67 'TWAS THE NIGHT BEFORE CHRISTMAS

68 LOOK UP!

69 A NORDIC NOËL

70-71 FESTIVE FIREWORKS

72-73 "GOD JUL"

74-75 "FRÖHLICHE WEIHNACHTEN"

76-77 "FELIZ NAVIDAD"

78-79 CHRISTMAS DOWN UNDER

80-81 "GLEÐILEG JÓL"

82 PIÑATA PARTY

83 GRANDPA FROST

84-85 A FESTIVE FEAST

86-87 LET'S PLAY

88-89 PARTY TIME

90 MERRY CHRISTMAS!